DK DORLING KINDERSLEY *READERS*

BEGINNING **1** TO READ

A Bed for the Winter

Written by Karen Wallace

London • New York • Sydney • Delhi
Paris • Munich • Johannesburg

A fluffy-tailed dormouse
stops by a meadow.

Cold rain is falling.
Soon snow will be coming.

The dormouse is looking
for somewhere to sleep.
She needs a bed for the winter.

meadow

A squirrel gathers leaves
high in a tree.
He makes his nest warm
for the cold winter weather.

nest

But a nest in the treetops
is too high for a dormouse.
The dormouse looks up,
then scurries by.

A queen wasp sleeps
under an oak stump.
She has squeezed through
a crack in the rotten wood.

stump

But a crack in an oak stump
is too small for a dormouse.
The dormouse looks in,
then scurries by.

A golden-eyed toad sleeps
under a stone.
It is muddy and wet and
the toad's skin is cold.

But it's too wet for a dormouse
under a stone.
The dormouse looks in,
then scurries by.

A mother brown bear
sleeps in a den.
She is furry and warm.
She stretches and yawns.

den

The dormouse looks in.
The bear's teeth are huge!
The dormouse trembles ...
then scurries by.

cave

Bats hang in a cave and cling to the rock. They huddle together and sleep through the winter.

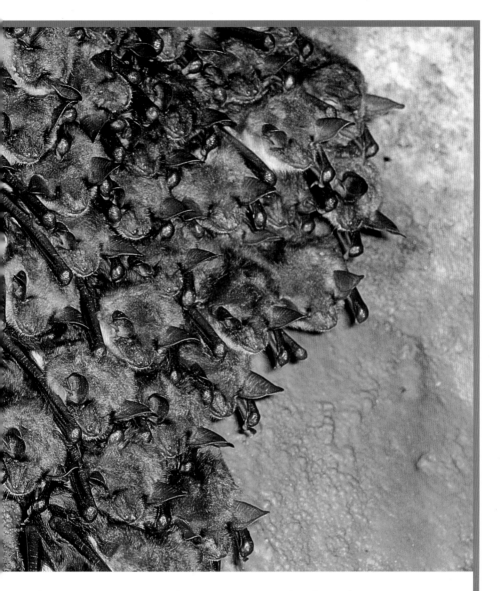

The cave is damp and dark.
It's too cold for a dormouse.
The dormouse looks in,
then scurries by.

A family of rabbits
hop into their burrow.
They live underground
when the weather is cold.
But there are too many rabbits
to make room for a dormouse.

burrow

The dormouse
looks in,
then scurries by.

An owl
with sharp claws
flies over the meadow.
He is hungry
and watchful.
He is hunting
for mice.

The owl swoops!
The dormouse
hides in a bush.

Where can she find
a safe bed
for the winter?

A deer comes to the meadow.
She nibbles the grass.
Her coat has grown thick
for the cold winter weather.

The dormouse shivers in the wind,
then scurries by.

A storm is coming.
The sky has turned black.

Bees fly home
to their hive.

hive

Ants run to their nest.

The dormouse waits
under a branch
for the storm to pass by.
Where can she find
a safe bed for the winter?

A snake slides through the grass.
He has hungry black eyes.
He stares at the dormouse.
His tongue flicks in and out.

The dormouse
is trapped.
She's too scared
to move.

The snake slithers closer.
His forked tongue comes nearer.

BOOM!
Thunder rumbles.
CRACK!
Lightning flashes.

The snake stops for a second,
then shoots into the grass.

The dormouse runs
through the meadow.
Her heart pounds like a drum.
She climbs up a tree trunk.

tree trunk

She crawls into a hole.
She finds a place
that is safe and dry!

Snow falls on the meadow.
The ground is
frozen and hard.
Snug in the tree hole,
the dormouse is sleeping.
Her long, fluffy tail
is wrapped tightly
round her.

Her search is over.
The dormouse is safe.
At last she has found
her bed for the winter!

Picture Word List

meadow

cave

nest

burrow

hive

stump

den

tree trunk